This book belongs to:

....

....

Retold by Monica Hughes
Illustrated by Daniel Howarth

Reading consultants: Betty Root and Monica Hughes

Marks and Spencer p.l.c.
PO Box 3339
Chester, CH99 9QS

shop online
www.marksandspencer.com

ISBN 978-1-84461-567-4
Printed in China

First Readers

The Enormous Turnip

MARKS &
SPENCER

Helping your child to read

First Readers are closely linked to the National Curriculum. Their vocabulary has been carefully selected from the word lists recommended by the National Literacy Strategy.

Read the story

Read the story
to your child
a few times.

So the girl pulled the boy.
The boy pulled the old woman.
The old woman pulled the old man.
But they couldn't pull up the
enormous turnip.
So the old man said to his
donkey and his goat,
"Can you help me pull up my
enormous turnip?"

20

Follow your finger

Run your finger under
the text as you read.
Your child will soon begin to
follow the words with you.

Look at the pictures
Talk about the pictures. They will help your child to understand the story.

The girl pulled the boy.

21

Have a go
Let your child have a go at reading the large type on each right-hand page. It repeats a line from the story.

Join in
When your child is ready, encourage them to join in with the main story text. Shared reading is the first step to reading alone.

Once upon a time there was an old man.
The old man had a garden.
The old man had some seeds.
They were turnip seeds.
The old man planted the turnip seeds in his garden.

The old man had some seeds.

Every day the old man watered
his seeds.
All the turnips began to grow.
But one turnip began to grow
more than the others.
The turnip got bigger and bigger.

The turnip got bigger and
bigger.

very day the turnip got bigger and
gger and bigger.

he old man was happy.

"Look at my enormous turnip," he said.
"We can eat turnip for tea."

The old man was happy.

One day the old man said,
"Today I will pull up my
enormous turnip."
So the old man pulled.
But he couldn't pull up the
enormous turnip.
So the old man said to the old woman,
"Can you help me pull up my
enormous turnip?"

The old man pulled.

So the old woman pulled the old man.
But they couldn't pull up the
enormous turnip.
So the old man said to the boy,
"Can you help me pull up my
enormous turnip?"

The old woman pulled the
old man.

So the boy pulled the old woman.
The old woman pulled the old man.
But they couldn't pull up the
enormous turnip.
So the old man said to the girl,
"Can you help me pull up my
enormous turnip?

The boy pulled the old woman.

So the girl pulled the boy.
The boy pulled the old woman.
The old woman pulled the old man.
But they couldn't pull up the
enormous turnip.
So the old man said to his
donkey and his goat,
"Can you help me pull up my
enormous turnip?"

The girl pulled the boy.

So the donkey and the goat pulled and
pulled.
The girl pulled and pulled.
The boy pulled and pulled.
The old woman pulled and pulled.
The old man pulled and pulled.
They pulled and they pulled and …

They pulled and they pulled.

out came the enormous turnip.

When the turnip came out, the
old man fell on the old woman.
The old woman fell on the boy.
The boy fell on the girl.
The girl fell on the goat and
the donkey.

24

Out came the enormous
turnip.

The old man was happy.
"Look at my enormous turnip," he said.
"Now we can eat turnip for tea."

So the goat and the donkey and the
girl and the boy and the old
woman and the old man all had
turnip for tea.

"We can eat turnip for tea."

Look back in your book.
Can you read these words?

man

woman

boy

girl

turnip

donkey

goat

Can you answer these questions?

What did the old man plant in his garden?

What did the old man try to pull out?

Who had turnip for tea?

First Readers

(subject to availability)

Beauty and the Beast
Chicken Licken
Cinderella
The Elves and the Shoemaker
The Emperor's New Clothes
The Enormous Turnip
The Gingerbread Man
Goldilocks and the Three Bears
Hansel and Gretel
Jack and the Beanstalk
Little Red Riding Hood
The Princess and the Pea
Rapunzel
Rumpelstiltskin
Sleeping Beauty
Snow White and the Seven Dwarfs
The Three Billy Goats Gruff
The Three Little Pigs
The Ugly Duckling